First published 2012 Parragon Books, Ltd.

Copyright © 2018 Cottage Door Press, LLC
5005 Newport Drive, Rolling Meadows, Illinois 60008
All Rights Reserved

10 9 8 7 6 5 4 3 2 1

ISBN: 978-1-68052-451-2

Parragon Books is an imprint of Cottage Door Press, LLC.
Parragon Books® and the Parragon® logo are registered trademarks of Cottage Door Press, LLC.

The Princess and the Pea

Illustrated by Dubravka Kolanovic

PaRRagon

Once upon a time, there was a lonely prince. He lived in a big castle with beautiful rooms and a pretty garden.

But he wasn't happy because he didn't have someone special to share them with.

"If only I could find a lovely princess to marry," sighed the prince.

The king and queen did their
best to help. They held balls so the
prince could meet princesses from
all the nearby kingdoms.

The prince danced with tall
princesses and small princesses.

He talked to
LOUD princesses
and **proud**
princesses.

He met all kinds of princesses ...

but none of them was quite right.

After a while, the king and queen ran
out of princesses for their son to meet.

"Maybe it's time you went looking for
a bride," suggested the queen.

So the prince packed a bag, saddled
his horse, and waved goodbye to the
king and queen.

"Good luck!" said the king.
"Come back soon!"

The prince traveled far and
wide, and searched high and low
for the princess of his dreams.

Along the way, he met lots of lovely princesses.

Princess Grace loved
to dance, but her twirling
made the prince dizzy.

Princess Ginger loved to
cook, but her cakes made
the prince chubby.

Princess Flora loved to smell as pretty as a flower,
but her perfume made the prince sneezy.

ACHOOOO!

Maybe I'm just too fussy, thought the prince. But in his heart, he knew he hadn't met the princess of his dreams. So he headed back to the castle.

When he got home, the king and queen greeted the prince happily.

"I haven't found a princess yet," he sniffed sadly. "I guess I never will."

"Don't be silly," said the queen, "the right girl will come along soon."

That night, there was a terrible storm.
Thunder boomed so loudly that it
rattled the castle's windows.

RATTLE, TATTLE!

Lightning shook the table as the prince
and his parents sat down to eat their dinner.

The prince was about to help himself to dinner, when suddenly, they all heard a loud ...

RAT-A-TAT-TAT!

Someone was knocking on the door!

"Who could be visiting us on a night like this?" asked the queen.

The prince opened the door and found a very wet girl standing there.
Raindrops ran down her muddy cloak, making a puddle at her feet.

Drip!

Drop!

Drop!

Drop!

Drip!

Drip!

Drop!

The girl pushed back her hood and wild curls tumbled out.

"Hello," she said with a smile. "I got lost on my way home and wondered if I could stay here for the night. My name is Princess Polly."

She didn't look much like a princess. But princes must always be polite, so he invited her inside.

Soon the princess was warm and dry.

All night long, rain fell plippety-plop, plippety-plop on the castle roof. But the prince hardly noticed, because he was too busy talking to Princess Polly.

She was pretty and funny and kind. Princess Polly was everything the prince had hoped to find in a princess.

By the end of the evening,
the prince had fallen in love!

But the queen wanted to be sure that the girl really was a princess.

The queen told the servants to pile a bed high with mattresses. They heaved one on top of another until they had no more mattresses left. Then they placed a pillow and quilt right at the top.

Underneath the mattress at the very bottom, the queen placed a teeny, tiny pea.

Only a real princess would be able to feel something so small through all those mattresses!

When the queen showed Princess Polly to her bedroom, the girl gazed up at the tower of mattresses but didn't say anything. She was just grateful to have a bed for the evening.

"Good night," said Princess Polly.

"Sleep tight," whispered the queen.

Then Princess Polly changed into her nightgown and climbed right to the top of the pile of mattresses, and snuggled under the quilt.

The next morning, Princess Polly came down to breakfast with dark circles under her eyes.

She let out a great big YAWN!

"How did you sleep, my dear?" asked the queen.

Princess Polly burst into tears.

"I'm afraid I couldn't sleep a wink. There was something lumpy and bumpy in my bed. It kept me awake all night long!"

To Princess Polly's surprise, the queen clapped her hands with delight.

"So she is a **real** princess!" the queen cried.

The prince was overjoyed.

"Will you marry me, Princess Polly?" 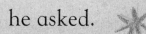 he asked.

"Yes!" squealed the princess.

And they all lived happily ever after!

The End